The Magical Tale of Easter Bunny Dust®
An Easter Tradition

Written by: Patricia Cardello

Illustrated by: Manuela Soriani

This book Belongs to: _____

I began my Easter Bunny Dust Tradition on: _____

N & J Publishing
New York

Once upon a time, in a small village called Faraway, there lived a young girl. She lived in a cottage on the edge of the forest, with her mother, father and younger brother.

Her brother was a few years younger, so it was up to her to teach him right from wrong, good from bad, now from never, and **would you please hurry up!**

They liked to play in the forest behind the cottage because there was so much to see and do there.

Just the day before, new baby ducklings hatched near the pond. And now that it was spring, there were many more new and exciting things to see. Spring was always about *new*. New flowers and baby animals and new birds, too.

The girl made a wreath from the dandelions that dotted the lawn. She put it on her head at a slightly crooked angle.

"Do you like my Easter bonnet?" she asked her brother.

Her brother nodded his head and smiled. "I'm glad Easter is tomorrow," he said. "*I hope the Easter bunny finds us this year. I sure would like to see the Easter bunny—just once.*"

The girl took his hand. "I don't know if that will happen, but we will hope for it. Let's go into the woods and pick flowers," she said. "Mother can put them on the windowsill. I'll tell her you picked them just for her."

When the basket was nearly filled with flowers, the girl had an idea. "Let's go on a treasure hunt," she suggested.

"What kind of treasure hunt?" asked her brother.

"Anything can be a treasure," she explained. "if it's something special or something new and pretty, it can be a treasure."

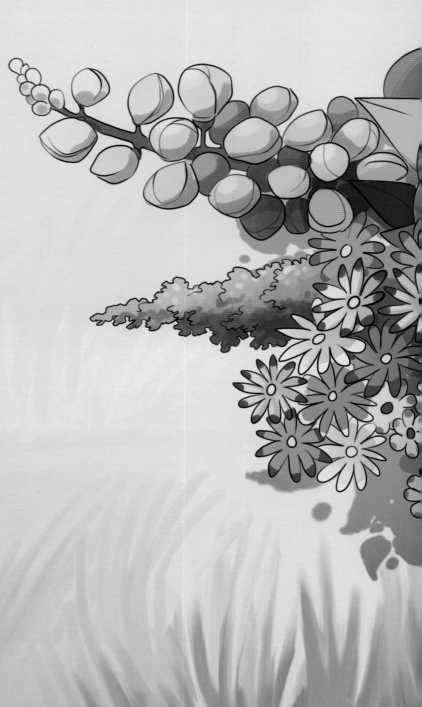

The boy ran around a tree and looked on the ground. He picked up a pinecone. "Is this a treasure?" he asked.

"I think it should be," she said. "Look how perfect it is, like a tiny Christmas tree." She dropped it into the basket.

They walked farther and continued to add to the treasures. A bird's nest that had fallen from a tree. A handful of acorns forgotten by the squirrels. A pretty blue feather. A shiny smooth stone. The boy now believed everything was a treasure and the basket was rapidly filling up.

Suddenly the girl stopped and leaned over to examine something on the ground.

"What is it?" asked her bother. "Is it a treasure?"

It was a small yellow pouch with a pretty tie.

The boy was squirming with delight. His voice was filled with excitement as he asked, "Can we open it? Can we open it?"

I think we must," his sister said seriously. "But let's make a wish first. Maybe whatever's inside is magic. Let's wish for something we really want to happen. Just one thing."

They sat on the ground studying the pouch and thinking.

The boy spoke quietly. "I can only think of one thing I really want, but you may think it's foolish."

"No, I won't," his sister said firmly, "and just to prove it, you can make the one wish, and no matter what it is, we won't change it."

The boy cleared his throat. "Here it is, then. *I want the Easter bunny to come to our house this year—and I want to see him.*"

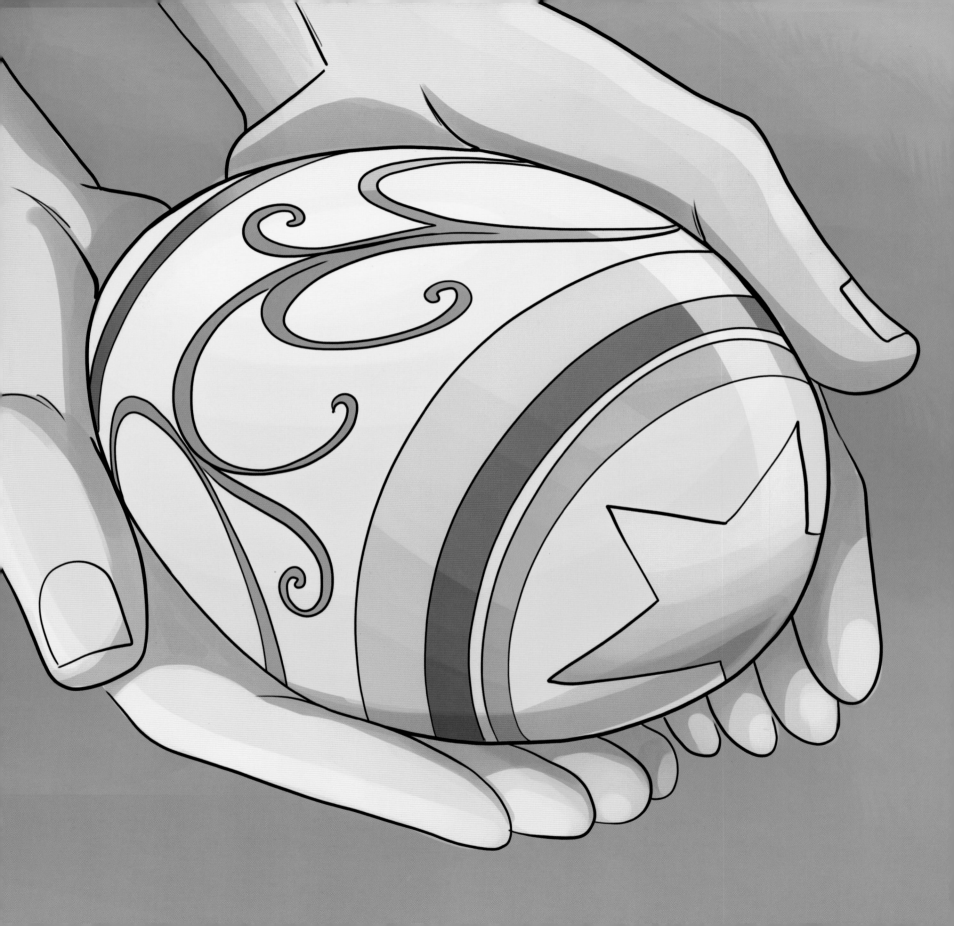

His sister was delighted and she hugged him. "That's a wonderful wish! Now let's see what's in the pouch."

She pulled the drawstring and reached inside. She felt something kind of round and warm. She lifted it out and gasped. It was an egg - the most beautiful egg they had ever seen.

My goodness," she cried. She cradled it carefully in her hand. She turned it over. She let her brother hold it. They examined every inch of it. It sparkled and glittered and glowed. It was blue and purple and pink and yellow, with silver and gold stripes and stars. They were speechless.

Let's take it home," the girl said. "Where is the pouch?"

They searched everywhere. But the pouch was nowhere to be found. They tucked the egg carefully amongst the flowers and treasures, and hurried home. The egg, bouncing gently as they walked.

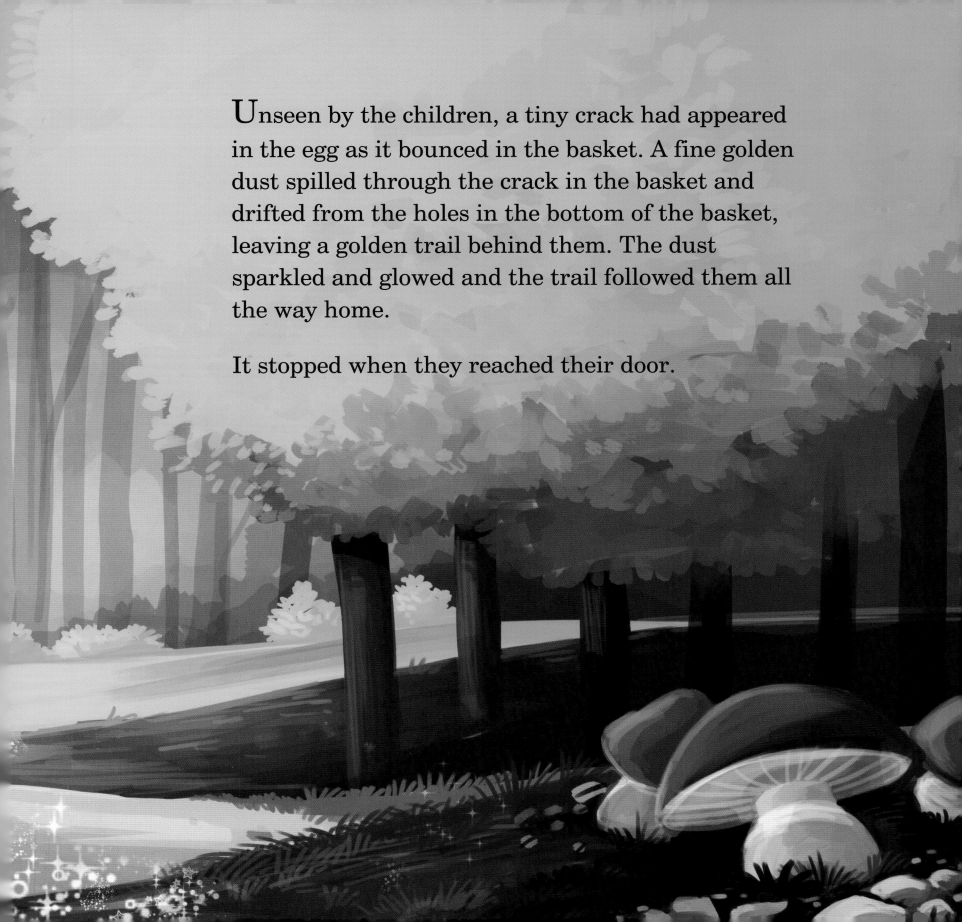

Unseen by the children, a tiny crack had appeared in the egg as it bounced in the basket. A fine golden dust spilled through the crack in the basket and drifted from the holes in the bottom of the basket, leaving a golden trail behind them. The dust sparkled and glowed and the trail followed them all the way home.

It stopped when they reached their door.

The children slept peacefully that night, dreaming of ducks and flowers and beautiful shining eggs.

When they woke in the morning, they ran to the kitchen where they heard a scratching noise on the door.

They opened the door and before them was a fluffy, white Easter bunny sitting on their porch. Colorful baskets of treats were on the steps. The bunny wiggled its nose, turned, then looked back at them one more time, and hopped away. The boy smiled and clapped his hands.

He got his wish. He really did.

In one of the baskets was the missing yellow pouch, with traces of the fine sparkly dust inside. There was a note attached to it. The girl took the note and they sat on the steps while she read it.

Sprinkle on the ground at night,
the moon will make it sparkle bright,
The Easter bunny hops and roams,
this will lead him to your home.

To Bob, Nicole & Jenna
In memory of Mom & Dad!

First Edition
ISBN: 978-0-9833662-3-2
Illustrations by Manuela Soriani – arcemproject@yahoo.it

"Easter Bunny Dust" and
"The Magical Tale of Easter Bunny Dust - An Easter Tradition"
are registered trademarks of PAC Jennic Inc.

Printed in China

N & J Publishing
200 North End Avenue, NY, NY 10282, 212-260-7075, 212-330-7708
nandjpublishing@aol.com,www.themagicaltales.com